Doctor Crotchet's Symphony

Doctor Crotchet's Symphony

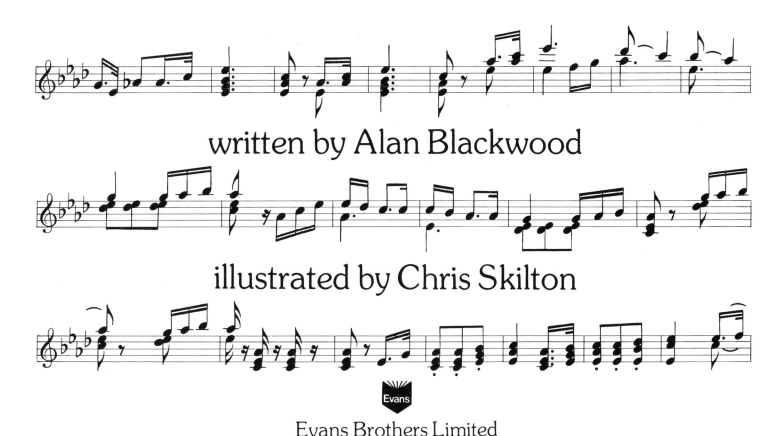

written by Alan Blackwood

illustrated by Chris Skilton

Evans Brothers Limited

Doctor Crotchet was writing a symphony.
It was going to be the biggest, longest, loudest symphony
in the world.
At last he finished it. He felt very proud.

Doctor Crotchet took the score of his
symphony to the Music Academy. He
showed it to the orchestra. They laughed
and would not play his symphony.
"All right," thought Doctor Crotchet.
"Just you wait," and off he went to see his
friend Professor Nut.

Professor Nut lived in an old house in the oldest part of town. The Professor invented things.
Doctor Crotchet knocked on his door. "Invent me an orchestra to play my symphony please," he said to Professor Nut.

"Hum. Ha. Now let me see," said Professor Nut. "Ah yes, I think I know what to do. We can record all the instruments on my tape recorder. You play them one by one. I'll make it sound as if you are playing all the instruments at once."

So Doctor Crotchet brought all the instruments he needed to Professor Nut's laboratory.

"I'll just fix up this tape," Professor Nut told him.
"That's it. Ready when you are!"
Doctor Crotchet took a violin and began to play the violin part of his symphony.

a cello

Doctor Crotchet
played a viola,

and a double bass.

He blew into a piccolo, a flute, a clarinet, an oboe

and a bassoon.

He blew even harder into a trumpet,

a trombone,

a French horn

and a tuba.

He thumped a kettle drum, crashed the cymbals,

whacked a gong
and whammed
the tubular bells.

He strummed a harp,

hammered at a piano

and went crazy at the organ.

"Is that all then?" asked Professor Nut.

"That's everything," gasped Doctor Crotchet.

"Right," said the Professor, "I'll fix the amplifiers on the roof. Then we'll play back your symphony so that everybody can hear it."

And that's what they did ...

Published by Evans Brothers Limited
Montague House Russell Square
London, W.C.1.

Text © Alan Blackwood 1977
Illustrations © Chris Skilton 1977
First published 1977

Printed in Great Britain by Hazell, Watson & Viney Ltd,
Aylesbury, Bucks.

ISBN 0 237 44869 6   PRA 5341